HORROR CIRCUS

BY

STEVEN FARKAS

DEAD CROW BOOKS

ADELPHIA, NJ

© 2021 Steven Farkas

All rights reserved. No part of this book may be reproduced, stored in a retrieval system, or transmitted in any form or by any means without prior written permission of the publisher, except by a reviewer who may quote brief passages in a review to be printed in a newspaper, magazine or journal

This is a work of fiction, any resemblance to actual persons is coincidence.

ISBN: 9798545566945

For my family and friends

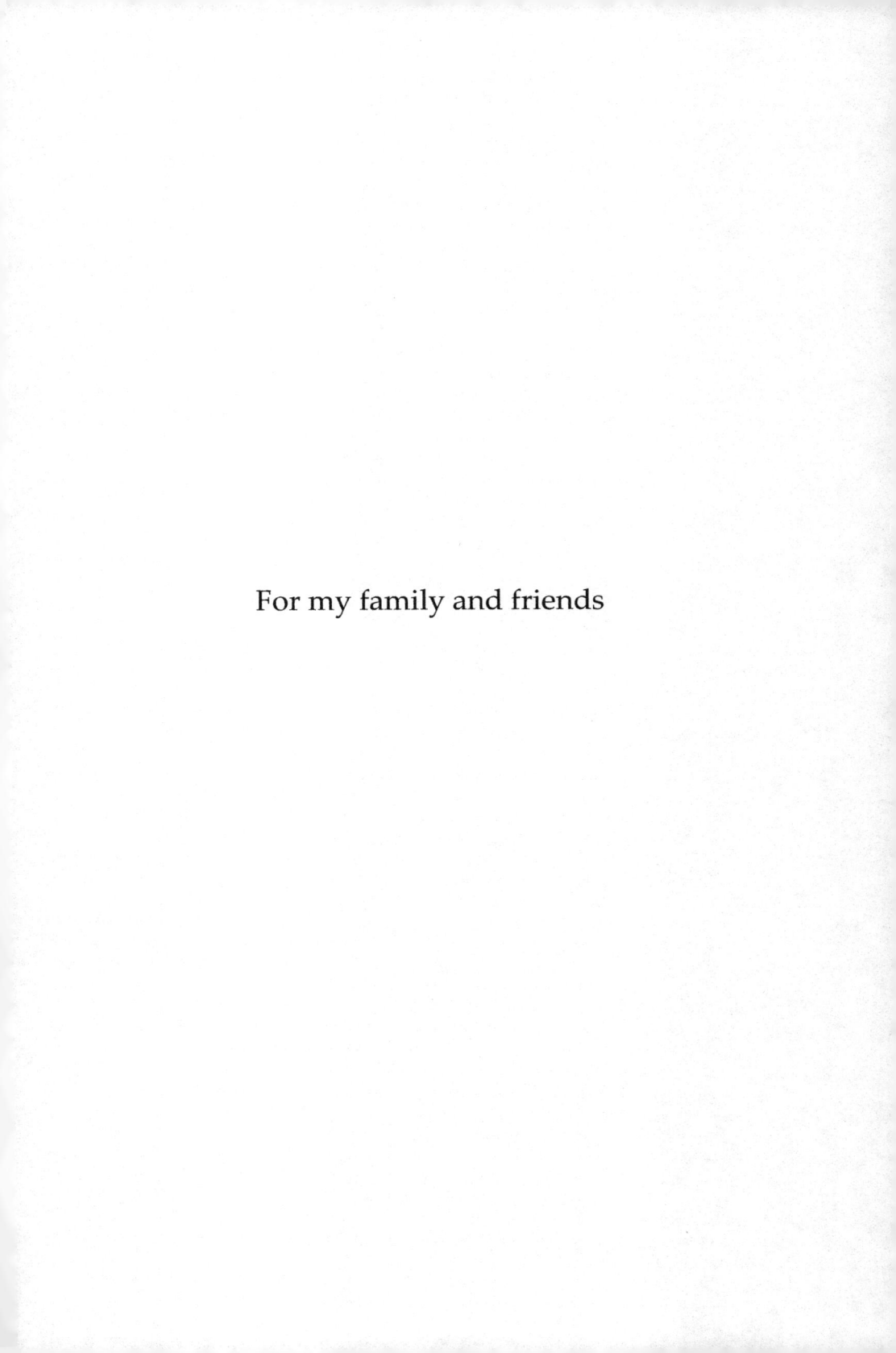

STEVEN FARKAS
HORROR CIRCUS

DEAD CROW BOOKS

1.
Here Comes The Horror Circus, Again

The trucks of the Big Top Circus rumbled down Center Street in the small New Jersey town of Darkside. They were headed to the county fairgrounds on the edge of town.

The people of the town watched through their windows with nervousness and a little bit of fear as the trucks rolled past. Every year the circus arrived in their town, and every year it brought with it strange and often violent occurrences. Most of the citizens in Darkside didn't want the circus in their town anymore. They fought to stop it from coming each year, and each year it still arrived every Summer.

Every year since the first time the circus arrived in town with the first of the odd events, the people lobbied the county government to withhold access to the county fairgrounds from the circus. However, the county retorted that the county was a poor county and needed the economic income the circus brought with it. People from all over came to see the sideshow freaks, ride the rides, and watch the show under the big tent. They brought money with them, and so who cares if it created problems for one little town.

Even the small businesses, the bookstore, restaurant, gas station, and thrift store, in town supported the circus. They did so even though it brought with it strange occurrences like murder, someone set on fire, and clowns following children home in full costume; because they needed the income. This led to a serious split in the town. Because of all the oddities that occurred during the long week, many in town referred to the Big Top Circus as a Horror Circus. But the business owners would reprimand those people hoping not to offend the performers.

As the last of the trucks passed through the town and entered the fairground, there was already a small group of townsfolk who decided they needed to meet and discuss what to do about getting rid of the Big Top once and for all. They knew it would have to be in secret and away from the prying eyes of those neighbors who were on the other side of the situation.

They nominated one person to go to the pastor and secretly ask to use the church basement for such a meeting. Zander Flynn headed to the local church like a spy to follow through with his secret mission.

"Pastor," Zander said as he walked up the steps of the church. "Robert, wait up."

Pastor Robert Binch turned to see Zander heading towards him.

"Zander, what do you need?" Pastor Robert asked.

"Can we talk somewhere not out in the open?" Zander asked.

"Sure, let's go to my office," Pastor Robert said.

The two entered the office off to the side of the church entrance. They sat and at first just joked back and forth about everyday things. Then the pastor wanted to know why Zander needed to talk in secret.

"It's about the circus," Zander said.

"I see," Pastor Robert said.

Robert was squarely on the side of those in the town who had problems with the circus being allowed to use the county fairground in town. He also knew there were a few important people in the town who supported the circus, all of them business owners, and all of them local elected town officials.

"You know this can't go on," Zander said. "I mean one year a clown follows children around, another people are set on fire, murder, death on rides, it's gotten out of control."

"So what do you want from me?" Pastor Robert asked.

"We need a space to plan," Zander said.

"Plan for what?" Pastor Robert asked.

"You may not want to know," Zander said.

"I see," Pastor Robert said. "Well, the basement seems like a perfect space."

"I was hoping you would say that," Zander said.

2.
Creepy Clown

Howard Silk sat in front of the mirror as he put his clown make-up on. He was by all standards a small and undesirable man. There was little about him that anyone would notice when he was out of costume. But when he put on his clown outfit, he felt noticed, he felt like he was somebody.

Howard became Grinner the clown when made up. He was named that because of the huge grin painted onto his face. But behind that painted grin there laid a demon in waiting.

He had joined the Big Top Circus after spending years first as a used car salesman yearning to be someone greater. The call of the circus came as he was in the middle of a sale to a tall lanky man with long white hair and an ill-fitting suit. The man was Gerald Ingram, owner and proprietor of the Big Top circus.

18 * Steven Farkas

Ingram had explained all about his circus while purchasing his large used cherry red 1980s Cadillac. Howard listened deeply and could see himself as doing something greater with his life, his depressing little life.

He stared into the mirror as he painted the smile onto his face. Behind that smile there hid something deep and dark. There he hid a weakness, a desire that made him afraid of himself. That weakness was the impetus to be a clown.

They had arrived in the town of Darkside the day before and this night was the next to last of the five days they would stay there. That night he scanned the crowd as he juggled and made pratfalls during his routine. He had never acted on his weakness, but there in Darkside he thought it might be easy to get away with doing a dark deed.

He spotted his mark half-way up in the

stands under the Big Top tent. The boy was laughing and having a great time. A cheery child with rosy cheeks. Howard was so distracted that he missed his pratfall and just about screwed up the entire performance.

The show ended and the tent emptied out in good time. Howard made his way back to his mirror where on any other night he would sit and remove his makeup. But this night he kept his entire costume on, clown makeup included.

He walked out of the tent and looked around the parking lot. It didn't take him long to spot his mark who was walking with what looked like his older sister down towards the main road of town. He knew the family must live close by, and that the parents allowed the siblings to walk together, but alone.

At this point he decided to follow the two and see where they are going. He knew his white outfit would stand out in the streetlights so he would have to stay in the shadows.

He crept slowly beyond the lights as he followed the boy and his older sister. They stopped and looked around. He stopped, worried they sensed his presence. The older sister looked right in his direction. As he stood perfectly still, he worried that she was looking straight at him.

Then, the older sister grabbed her brother and took off running dragging the boy behind. Howard then knew for sure he had been made. The sister, in her teens, began screaming for her dad as she ran. Howard froze, he wasn't sure if he should run after the two, or race back to the circus.

"Dad! There's a creepy clown following us!" she shouted.

"Oh fuck," Howard said to himself.

As Howard turned to run, he was broadsided by a large man and knocked to the ground. The man began banging his head on the ground. Then he dragged him into the street and slammed his head on the pavement until his brains began to leak out turning the black top red and sticky with brain matter until Howard laid there gurgling.

"Follow my kids, die motherfucker, die!" the dad shouted as he continued to wreak havoc on what remained of Howard's body.

People began to come out of their houses after hearing all the ruckus outside. They saw their neighbor beating what looked like a clown to death in the middle of the street in front of their houses.

"Joe!" a neighbor yelled. "What the hell are you doing?"

"Leave it alone Betty," Joe said. "This motherfucker was following my kids home from the circus. This creepy fucking clown son of a bitch."

"Joe, he's gonna die," another neighbor yelled.

"Bill, ask me if I care," Joe said.

"I'm calling the police," Betty said as she started dialing on her cellphone.

"Don't you dare Betty!" Joe shouted.

"Hello, we need help on Center Street," Betty said into the phone.

Joe let go of the creepy clown and began to run back to his house. Bill tried to get in his way to stop him, but he knocked Bill over and continued on until he made it home.

"Damn it Joe, you can't run away from this!" Bill shouted.

The front door of the house slammed shut as the police car and ambulance pulled up to the scene. Bill and Betty explained what they had seen.

The police went to the house and knocked on the door. When there was no answer they knocked the door down. Gun shots rang out, one of the police officers was struck in the head blowing most of it off. The other officer jumped Joe almost simultaneously and managed to cuff him.

Howard survived, but he spent the rest of his days staring into the abyss while drooling on himself.

This led to the first time the people of the town of Darkside tried to stop the Big Top circus from returning, but a failed attempt to be sure.

3.
The Lion, The Witch, And The Blood Covered Metal Cage

One of the popular parts of the circus was the lions. Their trainer was a younger woman who seemed to mesmerize the lions into doing whatever she wanted them to do. Wherever the circus went, the crowds cheered at the lions and their performance.

It was no different in Darkside. The crowd in the main tent loved to watch the powerful animals and their young trainer. She didn't even use a whip, just called out commands and the lions did what they were supposed to do.

It was the day after one of the clowns had been beaten nearly to death by a local man in town. The young woman was angry about her friend's beating. She sat in her trailer and fuming about the occurrence decided she would do something about getting revenge.

She quietly left for the local police station where she knew the killer was sitting in a cell. She walked the street in the dark, looking at the windows of the houses she passed. She could often see the families sitting in their living rooms watching television. None of them even noticed her watching them as she passed by. They were too busy staring blindly at the television as it glowed upon their dull faces.

She entered the Darkside police department just as casual as could be and walked up to the intake officer behind the plexiglass.

"Open the door and let me in," she said.

The officer looked at her oddly and asked, "What did you say?"

"I said open the door and let me in," she said again.

Her eyes began to glow. She moved her hands back and forth and then pointed to the locked door.

"You will open the door and let me in," she said.

"I will open the door and let you in," the police officer responded. Then he went to the door, unlocked it, and stood aside as she entered.

She made her way to the cell in which the man who had beaten her friend was sitting. She then told the officer to unlock the cell. He did as she directed.

"What the hell? Who are you?" the man asked.

"I am Zelda," she said. "And you are Joe."

"How do you know my name?" Joe asked.

"I know everything about all the world and universe," Zelda said.

"What are you some kind of witch?" Joe asked.

"You could call me that," Zelda said.

"You're one of those freaks from the circus, that clown got what he deserved," Joe said.

"Silence!" Zelda shouted. "You will get up and follow me."

"The fuck I will," Joe said.

Zelda waved her hands, her eyes grew bright and glowing again. Joe stood up and walked out of the cell. Zelda told the officer to enter the cell. Once he did, she locked him in.

As they began to head towards the exit of the police station, several officers where entering.

"Where are you two going?" one officer said.

"What are you doing with him?" another officer said.

"He's mine, you will move aside and let us through," Zelda said.

The officers moved aside and the two left the police station and headed for the county fairgrounds and the circus. They walked past the houses as Zelda had done on her way to the police station. Once again, the families sat with their full attention to the television not seeing or knowing that Zelda and her captive ward had gone by their house.

They entered the fairground and made their way towards the lion's cages. Zelda opened one of the cages. Joe walked in and then she slammed the cage shut. The lion moved out of the shadows. Joe now released from Zelda's grip backed against the cage bars screaming.

The lion attacked, it was the last thing Joe ever saw.

The next morning the circus began to pick up stakes as it prepared to move along to the next town it was scheduled to be at. As the work of packing up was going on, a police car arrived at the fairground.

"What can I do for you chief?" Gerald Ingram asked.

"It seems Joe has been broken out of our police station," Roger Born, the chief of police said.

"Really, that's terrible," Gerald Ingram said. "You really need to do better chief."

"Well, it seems someone from your circus is responsible," the chief said.

"I highly doubt that," Ingram said.

"That's what one of my officers said," the chief responded.

Gerald peered over at Zelda's mobile home. "I don't believe it," he said.

"Well, me and my men are going to look around anyway," the chief said.

"Be my guest," Gerald Ingram said.

For nearly two hours the police searched for Joe. They passed the lion cages multiple times as one of the lions chewed on one of Joe's bones. They never found what they were looking for, including Zelda who seemed nowhere.

"Nothing chief?" Gerald asked.

The chief grumbled under his breath. The police left and the circus packed up and moved on to the next town on the schedule. But they would return the following year to be sure.

4.

The Bearded Woman Is Hungry

Amelia Zelot, otherwise known as the bearded woman, brushed her hair and her beard preparing for her show. She listened as the carnival barker shouted to the assembled crowd in front of the sideshow stage.

Then she heard her cue as the barker shouted, "The bearded woman!"

She walked down the darkened hall towards the flood lit stage. She blew on her freshly painted fingernails which were not fully dried yet. Then through the curtain and out onto the stage she went.

"Hello my lovelies," she said. "How are we tonight?"

The crowd first gasped, then smiled, and finally began clapping. Amelia loved the attention. She had always been different when she was a child and she knew it. Because of her overgrown facial hair she was brutally teased by both the boys and the girls at school. Eventually she was forced to leave school because her local town school system hated anyone different and viewed her as a distraction to the upright students. But now, she was a star.

At that point, as the clapping began to die down, Amelia noticed a group of young men who had not clapped and were staring menacingly in her direction. They were all conservatively dressed with tan pants, what looked like dress jackets and expensive shirts in the mold of Brooks Brothers.

"Well let's get started," Amelia said.

For the next half an hour she sang, intermittent with jokes. Most of the crowd seemed mesmerized by her voice and humility. All but the young men in the back.   Amelia kept herself aware of them, she knew they were born of entitlement and that meant they were trouble.

After Amelia finished her show, she reveled in the applause and then disappeared behind the curtain. Most of the crowd left, but the young men remained, looking angry and ready for violence.

When Amelia began to walk back to her trailer she could hear footsteps behind her. She knew it was the young men looking to beat her down just to prove their masculinity. She had dealt with haters like this all her life, she knew how to handle them.

She whipped around to face them. "Boys," she said. "What can I do for you?"

"We're not boys you freak of nature," One of the young men said. "We're real men."

"Oh, I see, real men huh," Amelia quipped.

"Yes, that's what I said," he replied. The other young men shook their heads and in low voices said, "Yeah."

"Well, well, well," Amelia said. "Good for you."

She turned away from them and continued walking towards her trailer. She heard the young men running towards her. She decided to vanish.

The men stopped in their tracks.

"Where'd she go?" one of them queried. They turned in circles looking for her.

Then before they could move another step they were set upon by a fast moving creature with long fangs. They were cut and drained of their blood. The fangs ripped the flesh wide open. They were all dead within a matter of minutes. Then Amelia wiped the blood from her lips and retracted her vampire fangs.

"Thank you, gentleman, I was quite hungry," Amelia said to her quarry. "There's always a bunch of entitled assholes to eat at every stop."

The morning came, the bodies were gone. In a matter of a day or so flyers would go up around Darkside asking for information on the missing young men. The townsfolk knew it was probably yet another horror to occur during the circus, but the circus continued anyway. The local businesses and the county where still making good money.

5.
Pyromaniac Imp

Abraham Scott was a little person born of two non-little people. His parents, especially his father, ignored and despised him for his unfortunate birth as something they thought of as a failure. To them he was grotesque and a sign they had angered God in some way. He was neglected most of the time as they simply couldn't handle what was their failure as they saw it.

He never finished his schooling and ran away from home at age fourteen to live alone on the street. After four years of scrounging to stay alive he came upon Gerald Ingram and the Big Top Circus. He joined right away and soon felt he had found his place in the universe and a real family.

Wherever the circus went he was the comic relief as a small clown among other little people who also performed as comical clowns. Of course the most liked part of their act was how many of them fit inside a car. Crowds loved it.

Abraham had always worn a chip on his shoulder about his size. He always felt people were laughing at him or making fun of him because he was a little person. That first year he was with the circus, they went to the town of Darkside where he became overwhelmed with his anger at society.

He found himself one afternoon in Darkside walking down the sidewalk. Store fronts were littered with flyers of missing young men. Abraham looked at each one as he passed them. He remembered some of the faces of the men. They had laughed at, pointed at him, and called him an imp.

"Look at the little imp," they would say.

As he looked at the faces, he would smile in happiness that they were gone. He suspected what had happened to them. He knew it had to be Amelia.

"Hey, there's the little imp," he heard someone say.

He looked around, and there were a bunch of teenagers pointing at him. He felt the anger welling up inside him. They just kept laughing for what felt like forever to Abraham. Then they just started walking away down a side street.

Abraham followed behind them watching where they were going. At first the teenagers didn't notice him and continued on their merry way. But he kept up behind them.

Then one of the girls stopped to tie her shoe and noticed Abraham was there just a few yards away.

"Guys," she said. "He's following us."

All of the teens stopped and turned around. Abraham stopped in his tracks. He didn't know what they were going to do, and he also didn't know what he was going to do.

"What are you doing imp?" one of the boys said.

"I'm not an imp," Abraham said. "The correct term is little person."

"Ha, the imp talks," the boy said.

At that point the girls in the group told the boy he should stop what he was doing. But he would not stop his offensive comments. Then the other boys started to join in. The girls decided to leave the boys there and move on. They were annoyed that the boys wouldn't stop being a bunch of asses.

"Why don't you just go back to the circus imp," one of the boys said, as they turned and decided to walk away with the girls.

Abraham couldn't stop the anger he felt. He noticed he was standing next to the local liquor store and he decided to get a bottle of whisky. He didn't drink, he had other plans.

When he walked up to the counter with his bottle, the man behind the counter gave him a strange look. Abraham had seen that look many times before. It was a look of shock and then fear and disgust.

"There a problem here?" Abraham asked.

"No, no problem," the man said. But the look was still in his eyes.

Abraham shocked himself with what he did next. He opened the bottle and tossed whisky on the man, then lit a match and tossed it at him, setting him on fire. The man ran around knocking down other bottles of high proof alcohol and spreading the fire through out the store. Abraham ran out of the burning store but not before he grabbed another bottle of whisky to finish his original plan of getting even with the teenagers.

It took him some time, but he eventually found the pack of teenagers who had ridiculed him. He only had one bottle of whisky, so he couldn't set everyone on fire, he would have to wait for the boy who started making fun of him to separate out from the rest.

As fire trucks raced past the teenagers walking down the street, they stopped to see where it was going. There was tons of smoke billowing into the sky.

"Whoa," one of the boys said. "We should check it out."

"Yeah," Abraham's main target said. "Just let me take a piss first."

The teens ran to check out the fire and left the other boy to find a dark spot on the street to relieve himself.

"Hey guys wait up," the boy said as he finished with a couple of shakes.

When he turned to run, there stood Abraham. In a flash he tossed the whisky on the boy, lit a match, and tossed it setting him on fire. Then he laughed and walked away loving every scream from the boy until the screams stopped.

Once again the circus was paid a visit by the police as they were packing up to leave Darkside. Once again nothing happened and the circus left. The townsfolk complained to no avail and the Big Top would return again the next Summer.

6.
Merry Go Round From Hell

The merry go round was a popular ride at the circus. Families with small children always used it every time they came. The kids would laugh, the parents would smile, and it just seemed to be a ride that they liked.

After a couple of years at the county fairground in Darkside New Jersey the circus had gotten a bad name. Luckily they had been protected by the powers that be since they brought people and money into the depressed town and county in the poorest, most rural, part of the state.

No one really cared, or noticed how creepy the ride operators looked. They always had old dirty looking clothes, matted hair, and dirty ballcaps with drawings of naked ladies on them. Anywhere else someone saw them they would cross the road to get away from them. But there at the circus, they just faded into the canvas.

On that day in Darkside things became a bit crazy with the rides. It started with the merry go round.

A young slender man called Bobby Boy by all of the circus entertainers and workers, ran the merry go round. He kept his head down and was quiet when running the ride. Until, that is, a burly dad decided to pick a fight with him.

He started complaining about the ride being too slow and Bobby just stayed quiet and calm. Then the man, pissed off he couldn't get a rise out of Bobby, slapped that hat right off of Bobby's head. Then the man and his daughter got on the ride anyway.

Bobby picked up his hat and put it back on. His eyes focused on the man and his kid. He started the ride up slowly as normal. Then he made it go faster, not terrible, but a bit faster than normal. Slowly he increased the speed. It went faster and faster. Suddenly people holding their little ones on the horses began to fall down from the speed. Then people began to fall off of the horses.

Bobby watched the man trying to hang on and keep his kid on the horse. Then Bobby pushed the ride to the limit. He wanted the man and his kid to suffer.

People were screaming and crying as they were thrown from the ride. Bobby watched, and when the man and his child flew off of the ride into the metal line markers, he smiled and slowed the ride down.

"Happy now mister," he said, looking at the man bleeding out on the ground and his child still in his arms, safe.

7.

Ferris Wheel Of Fear

The Ferris Wheel was running like it always had. A young woman ran the ride. Her name was Cheryl and she was a slight woman with blonde hair. She always wore jeans and a checkered shirt. She wasn't quite as dirty looking as the men, but she wasn't a trophy wife either.

As the Ferris wheel went around and Cheryl watched it go, she heard screaming coming from somewhere. She looked around to see where the sound was coming from.

Someone went running past her. She yelled out, "What's going on?"

"It's the merry go round!" the person shouted.

"The merry go round?" Cheryl said to herself.

She looked in the direction of the merry go round and noticed it was going awfully fast. She had never seen it move like that.

"Holy shit," she said.

Without knowing it she was leaning on the controls to the Ferris Wheel. The wheel began to speed up like the merry go round had done. Suddenly Cheryl heard screaming from behind her. She turned around and saw the Ferris wheel going very fast. All of a sudden people began flying out of their seat and falling to the ground.

"Oh my God, what the fuck!" Cheryl said. She didn't know what had happened.

"What the," she said.

She looked down at the controls and realized what she had done. She quickly slowed the wheel down, but five people had already fallen from the Ferris Wheel.

She sat on the ground in disbelief of what had happened. It would be the last day she worked for the Big Top Circus.

This was the first time an investigation was opened because of the deaths due to the malfunctioning rides as it had been viewed. But, the circus was simply fined, and the circus agreed to no longer have either of the two rides that had led to the deaths.

And once again the Big Top would return to Darkside.

8.

Side Show Freak Gang

The sideshow performers were a ragged lot. Many had been part of the circus for quite a few years. They were a very tight group as they were often referred to as freaks. Over time they began to own the term. Now they were wearing black leather jackets with a large logo on the back stating Sideshow Freak Gang.

The show that year in the town of Darkside was no different. While not working they would wander downtown wearing their jackets. The locals often moved away from them as they walked down the sidewalk. It didn't really bother the gang, they were used to people fearing them. They figured people always feared what they didn't know.

This time as they walked downtown in Darkside, things felt different. People didn't move aside, in fact they often made sure they shouldered someone in the gang. It was a surprise. People no longer looked at them with fear, but rather disdain.

"What's wrong with you?" the alligator man said after being pushed in the shoulder.

"You, you scum," the man who did the pushing said.

The alligator man, called that because of a skin condition which made his skin look dried and crackled and a slight green hue, gave the man the finger.

"Screw you," he said.

The man walked towards the gang, looking angry and ready for a fight. The rest of the gang moved to the front between the two.

"Do that again, I'll rip that finger off," the angry man said.

The alligator man, whose name was Will Beringer, immediately raised his finger again. The man reached through the gang to get a hold of Will's finger. The gang began punching the man as hard as each of them could to get him to back off when suddenly a gunshot range out. Will dropped to the sidewalk with a large hole in his forehead. The man continued to fire at all of the sideshow performers.

"Run, run for it!" one of them yelled.

The man was so busy taking out his anger from his terrible life by trying to kill people, he did not see the bearded woman come up behind him. She sank her fangs into his neck and ripped out his throat. Then removed his head quickly to be sure he would not turn.

The gang grabbed their dead friend quickly and ran for the fairground. The police arrived on the scene just after they had fled. They asked everyone near the scene if they had seen anything. No one said they had.

"How is that possible?" one of the officers said. "Someone had to of seen something."

But everyone in the crowd continued to say they saw nothing, perhaps out of fear or apathy. But whatever it was, they stayed silent.

"Anyone know who this is?" he asked. "Since there's no head, it's hard for me to tell."

The gang had taken the head with them. When they arrived back at the fairground, they made sure to bury the head somewhere where they thought it would not be found. They did not want anyone to come after Amelia. She had saved them this time and she deserved to be safe.

They brought Will's body to his trailer. They laid him down and wrapped him in cloth to prepare him for burning. They did not want anyone other than themselves to send him on to the next world.

9.
The Stampede of the Elephants

The elephants were paraded around the main tent of the Big Top Circus. People loved to see the giant animals. They certainly were a fan favorite.

Afterwards they stayed in a metal stable on the grounds. There were often protestors just outside the fairgrounds. They thought using animals in the circus was cruel and protested to stop the using of animals in circuses. So they protested every year the Big Top Circus arrived in town.

The workers did their best to care for the animals, but it was not a perfect situation. The Elephants did, of all the animals, seem the most independent. They did just about what they wanted, not controlled by either the witch or the vampire as with the other animals.

On the last night the circus was in town, one of the protestors came onto the fairground to get to the elephants. He wanted to free them from their situation.

As he crept across the field he noticed smoke and a terrible smell. He slowly moved towards the smoke. When he peered around the corner of one of the trailers, he saw a group of the sideshow performers circled around a bonfire. He couldn't tell for sure, but it looked like they were burning a body wrapped in a cloth.

"What the hell?" he said to himself.

He crept as close as he dared to go out of the fear of getting caught. He had heard of all the stories over the years about the strange and dangerous things that went on at the circus.

At that moment the elephants started moving around and making noise. The protestor dropped to the ground hoping no one had seen him when they turned away from the fire to look over at the elephant stable.

"What's with Nellie?" Anton asked. He was known as the Wolf Man because of how hairy his whole body was. He was also good friends with Will.

"I don't know," Zelda said. "She has a mind of her own."

Nellie seemed to be pointing at something in the grass. Anton noticed movement where she was pointing. Without saying anything he directed everyone else to the movement in the grass.

They slowly started to creep towards the protestor laying on the ground. He noticed they were moving in his direction. Fearing the stories and what he had witnessed for himself, he got up and took off running towards the street.

Nellie became agitated and broke through the stable. All of the other elephants followed her out onto the street.

The protestor raced towards the town center being followed by a herd of elephants. The sideshow performers had begged off the hunt to ensure the funeral pyre went out and didn't burn the circus up.

Nellie was gaining on the interloper as he got closer and closer to the center of town. She overtook him just as he was about to enter a store. She struck him hard and broke the windows of the shop.

People strolling downtown took off screaming as they saw the elephants stampeding down towards them. But, just as quickly as the stampede started, it stopped. Nellie halted her fellow elephants, and they walked back up the road towards the fairground. They made it back and calmly went back into the stable.

As with every other year, the police paid a visit to the circus before they left town. The murder, the elephants running through town, all seemed a good reason to suspect the circus as guilty. But there was no evidence they were involved in the murder since no one would talk, and the elephants did only little damage to a business which Gerald Ingram gladly paid to fix. The protestors death was just an act of God.

The Big Top Circus moved on, and would return to Darkside again.

10.
Big Top Killer

Willard Millhouse was an overweight awkward weirdo. He loved the Big Top Circus and watched with glee every year at the strange acts that occurred every Summer when the circus was in town.

He hated people. He was always treated badly by everyone in town because of how odd a person he was to them. The more pain and violence that occurred to those in town, the happier he was.

That year he decided to join in on the fun. When the circus arrived in town, he would do the deed. He would kill those who were the most horrible to him. If it looked like the circus had something to do with it, it would be simply wiped away since important business people would protect the circus and the money they made when it came to town.

The first night he paid a visit to the home of Ben Robbins. He was always calling him names and accusing him of stealing. None of it was true, but Willard was always an easy target to use when it was necessary to deflect attention from Ben's bad behavior.

Willard was in and out in just ten minutes leaving behind a blood soaked scene with Ben cut open from pubic area to throat.

Each of the five nights the circus was in town he did the same to someone who had treated him badly in one way or another. Sometimes he killed a man, like Ben, other nights he slit women the same exact way. One night he took out an entire family.

He was right about the circus becoming the target of the police investigation. He was also right that the business community closed ranks and protected the circus.

Even though virtually every business owner had treated Willard badly, he was careful to stay away from them. He knew if he started killing off the business community he would be caught.

While he was marginally disappointed that he could not kill those in the business community who treated him badly, he was grateful with the opportunity to exact his revenge on at least some of those who had treated him so awfully over the years.

11.

Scare Ground

The trucks parked in the county fairground. They had driven for the last ten hours to get to Darkside. But they had arrived again for another year. The people in town went back inside after the trucks had gone past and went into the fairground.

"They might as well call it the county scare ground," Rod Bender said jokingly to his customer.

Rod was cutting the hair of a man. He owned Rod's Place, the local barber shop. Even though he was a local businessman, the arrival of the circus didn't add to his income. People didn't come to get a haircut when they arrived in town to go to the circus. They did go to restaurants and gas stations, and even some shops. Those were the businesses that felt they needed the circus to come to town every year.

"Yeah, I guess you're right," Bill Richards said as Rod cut his hair. "But then again I'm not sure the businesses, including mine, could survive without that income during the week the circus is here."

Bill Richards owned Richards Family Restaurant. Because of how small and hidden away in the water gap Darkside was, there just wasn't enough business throughout the year. But the week the circus was in town his business made nearly half their yearly income in just that week.

"I get that," Rod said. "But at what point is it just not worth the damage done to our town to keep the circus here?"

"I know, It's a devil's bargain, but until something changes, it's a bargain I have to keep," Bill said.

"Well, I guess I don't know what the answer is," Rod said.

"Me neither," Bill said.

Bill got up from the chair, paid for the service, and left the barber shop. At that same time Zander Flynn entered.

"Meeting, tonight at the church, be there," he said. Then turned to walk out.

"Meeting for what?" Rod asked before Zander could get out the door.

"It's important, trust me," Zander said. "I think you're on our side."

"So it's about stopping the circus," Rod said. "We've tried everything, what's left to do?"

"Just say you'll come," Zander said.

"Okay, I'll come," Rod said.

12.

The Meeting In The Church Basement

They entered the church basement. Zander was waiting for everyone to arrive. He had been given the role of leader and he was playing it up to the hilt.

"Thank you all for coming," Zander said as people shuffled around to find a seat.

"As you know I asked you here to discuss the circus and how it's caused so many problems for our town," Zander said.

The crowd nodded too as he spoke. For most in the town of Darkside the Big Top Circus had been nothing but a problem. They dreaded the week that the circus was in town.

"What do we do about this scourge in our town every Summer," Zander said.

"Really, what can we do?" Rod asked. He kept to his word and showed up at the meeting.

"Thanks for coming Rod," Zander said. "It's a great question, what can we do?"

"No one seems to listen to us," a member said from the group.

"Well, we need to make them listen," Zander said.

"Bull, it's time to take things into our own hands!" a man shouted from the crowd.

"What exactly does that mean?" Pastor Robert asked from the back of the room.

"It means we take care of business, one way or the other, to get these so-called people out of our town," the man said.

"That sounds like violence," Pastor Robert said.

"Damn right, if need be," The man said.

"You know I can't support violence under any circumstance," Pastor Robert said.

"What's a matter pastor, you some kind of peacenick hippy boy?" The man said. People began to snicker and giggle.

"No, I'm a sensible feeling and intelligent human being," Pastor Robert said.

"You saying I'm not intelligent?" the man said.

"Take it however you want," Pastor Robert said.

"Okay folks, we're getting nowhere fighting with each other," Zander said.

"Who's fighting, I think we're all in favor of getting rid of these circus freaks however need be," the man said standing up and imploring the rest of the crowd to agree with him.

Many shook their heads in agreement with the large muscle bound, no neck, steroid taking, angry man egging them on.

Pastor Robert gave Zander a look as though he was telling him that he needed to get control of the meeting. He feared things could take a nasty turn and he did not want to see mob rule justice in his town. He certainly didn't want such anarchy to stem from his church basement.

"People, people, please let's calm down," Zander said, trying to settle down the raucous crowd being revved up by one man with no care about humanity.

"Why should we?" the man said. "These fucking circus freaks don't give a damn about what happens to us."

"Come on Terry, let's not be like this," Zander said.

Terry, the big steroid laden knucklehead who was causing the problem, made a fist and held it in the air.

"What's that for," Pastor Robert said.

"Solidarity for my people," he said.

Pastor Robert shook his head and gave a chuckle. "Your people? Who are you, Norma Rae?"

Terry gave a strange look at the pastor and said, "You calling me a girl?"

"No, no I'm not," Pastor Robert said. "A girl as you say, would have more common sense then you."

Terry pointed at the pastor and said, "Fuck you pastor."

"Pastor Robert said, "Nice talk in front of everyone here."

"Can we all just calm down here?" Zander

questioned, trying to lower the temperature in the room.

"Fuck you too," Terry said to Zander.

"That's about enough," Pastor Robert said.

"Sorry pastor, but I'm not sure Terry is wrong," Rod said.

"Thank you Rod," Terry said.

"I don't give a damn about you Terry, but I think we are going to have to take things into our own hands or nothing will happen," Rod said.

"I don't think that is advisable Rod," Pastor Robert said. "You are an important leader in this community, don't use that to create a violent mob."

The room became surly and every man and woman in the room were growing loud and angry. Pastor Robert knew there was going to be an explosion of violence. He told everyone to leave.

"Oh don't worry pastor, we're going," Terry said. "You wait and see, this is the final day we have to worry about the circus."

That was exactly what Pastor Robert feared.

13.

Burn It All Down

Terry led the march out of the church into the street. He then began telling everyone what to do.

"Let's burn it all down!" Terry shouted.

"Yes!" everyone shouted.

Terry directed the people to get any kind of burning fluid, gas, lighter fluid, anything that burns. He then told them to get anything they could light on fire. Most assumed they should grab their tiki torches, while others grabbed paper and sticks they could put cloth onto.

Everyone scattered to their homes looking for what they needed to light the entire circus up and burn it down once and for all. All the commotion and noise grew until the town could hear it, including those business leaders who depended on the circus to survive.

"What the hell is going on?" Bill, the owner of the local restaurant said to no one in particular.

He noticed most of his neighbors rooting through their houses and garages. It made no sense to him at first. Then, he began to realize his neighbors were planning something terrible. He felt he had to contact all the other business owners to help him stop it.

The mob reconvened in the center of town and followed Terry up the hill to the fairground. They entered the grounds as quietly as they could hoping the performers were all asleep.

At the same time Bill called every person he could to get out to stop the mob with a mob of their own. He urged them to get to the fairground as quickly as they could.

Terry and the others with him began to spread gas and lighter fluid around the circus tents and trailers. They were serious about setting the whole thing on fire no matter if they killed anyone or not.

As they were soaking down the entire area, they suddenly heard something coming up the hill towards them. Marching with Bill were those who needed the money from the week of the circus.

"What the hell," Terry said.

"It's Bill and the others," Rod said. "He must have known what we were doing."

"And how would that have happened," Terry said.

"What are you saying?" Rod asked. "You think I did it?"

"Well, you do own a business," Terry said.

"So, I supported you at the meeting," Rod

said. "Why don't you assume it was the pastor, or Zander. Do you see him here?"

Terry looked around. Rod was right, Zander was nowhere to be found. He had not followed Terry.

"Yeah, maybe," Terry said, not liking the fact that Rod had a point that didn't support Terry's theory.

"What do you mean maybe, I'm right here aren't I," Rod said.

Terry looked at Rod for a moment. "Yeah, yeah, okay," he said.

Together Terry and Rod pushed the mob to move faster. They both began to light the fuel on fire. The big tent began to burn, lighting up the sky.

"Jesus," Pastor Robert said as he noticed the light in the sky from his position at the church.

Bill noticed the fire as well. He yelled and pushed his fellow business owners to move faster and get up there to stop what was going on.

Terry turned away from the burning tent and saw the group coming up over the hill and into the fairground. He looked around at his mob still spreading the accelerant around.

"Damn it, we need to light it up now," he said.

Terry began running around as quick as he could with flame to light the fuel and set everything on fire. Bill saw him coming towards the trailers and took off after him.

"Terry, you don't want to do this!" Bill yelled.

"I'm pretty sure I do!" Terry yelled back at him.

"You'll go to jail!" Bill yelled.

"I doubt that!" Terry yelled back.

"I can assure you, you will!" Bill yelled as he closed the gap on Terry.

"No one in this town will convict me!" Terry shouted, he reached Amelia's trailer and lit it on fire.

Everyone stopped as they saw a dark specter move towards Terry. He turned around just as Amelia sunk her fangs into his throat, and then ripped it right out.

"Holy shit!" Rod shouted.

"What the fuck!" Bill shouted.

Everyone began to run away heading back out of the fairground and down the hill as fast as they could. Amelia wasted no time in attacking every person she could get to as they ran for safety.

Soon she was joined by the other so-called freaks of the circus as they fought back. They didn't care if they were from the mob or were a supporter. They simply struck out at anyone.

People accidently set fire to buildings as they went along. They would fall, release the accelerant and then Rod or someone else carrying fire in their hand would set the fuel on fire.

Soon the town was ablaze as blood ran in the streets. Darkside was wiped from the face of the earth. The news would report it as an explosion, or a town wide fire started from electrical shorts. Some just viewed it as terrorism or the work of God.

Decades later, few knew the real story of why Darkside was just a forest filled with burned pieces of former houses and businesses. But the Big Top Circus still roamed the country, one dark little town at a time.

Other Books By Steven Farkas

Vampire, Werewolf, Aliens, Quiet Suburban Cannibals, A Murderous Ex-Girlfriend, Killer Clown, Bigfoot, A Neighbor with a lot of anger, and others. This is a flash fiction collection of horror stories 800 words or less by Steven Farkas

A collection of creepy and scary stories from horror author Steven Farkas. Whether it's a house with a haunted history, a case of love and murder, or an evil force attacking children in a small 17th century town, this collection will terrify you.

THERE'S BLOOD IN THE SNOW

STEVEN FARKAS

There's Blood in the Snow deals with a father who has accidently killed his son while hunting. He goes on a killing spree to keep it a secret so his wife won't divorce him. What he unleashes into the world will kill many more.

STEVEN FARKAS

LOST INTO THE MADNESS

Thomas finds himself locked away in a sanitarium, put there by his sister. Supernatural events help him find his revenge. The reality of his world turns out to be shocking and terrifying. A great story of pulp horror.

Zombie Carnival

Jane and John find themselves orphaned slaves in a time when two thirds of the world are zombies or dead and the government of the US is gone. When the chance comes for freedom they take it, but they end up unleashing zombies on locals in a small New Jersey town.

The Zombie Rollerderby Chicks From Hell

Head banging flesh tearing gorefest The Zombie Roller Derby Chicks from Hell. Part One: a rabid disease breaks out during a roller derby bout in a NJ seaside town. It takes only hours to spread town wide. Part Two: the zombies lead by the derby zombies spread the disease throughout the state.

The Jesus Camp Zombie Bloodbath

The Jesus Camp Zombie Bloodbath is a terrifically terrifying piece of B-pulp horror. While learning to speak in tongues in a summer religious camp, the children turn into zombies. They're hungry and the counselors look tasty. In no time they are busy chewing down on the adults at the camp, police officers, and the local town.

A Murder in The Dark City

The Blue Blaze book series set in 2300s in a dystopian NYC after the fall of The United States. Blue Blaze is a private detective and former NYC police officer. He's also a robot. A series of pulp 1950's style hardboiled crime set 300 years in the future. James Cain meets Phillip K. Dick. Murder in the Dark City is the first book in the Blue Blaze series.

Strange Experiments

People are disappearing off of the streets. The city doesn't know who is involved in these disappearances. Blue Blaze is asked by the authorities to look into it, against their better judgement. Can Blaze figure out what's going on before another disappearance. THIS IS THE SECOND BOOK IN THE BLUE BLAZE SCIENCE FICTION SERIES

Spawn of The Wasteland

Spawn of The Wasteland is the third book in the Blue Blaze Science Fiction series by Steven Farkas. Young spawns, the children of robots are disappearing from the wasteland, the term used for a shanty town in what once was Central park in NYC where only robots live. Blue Blaze is asked by a friend to find their spawn who has gone missing. Blaze uncovers a large conspiracy at the root of the disappearances.

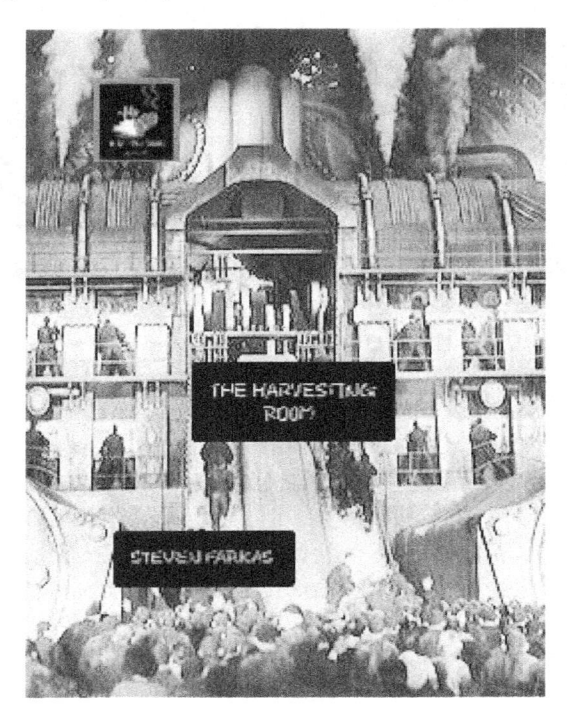

Welcome to the Harvesting Room is a speculative novella about an alternative dystopian U.S. future controlled by religious extremists following the Christian Party Movement and Sari Heilyn, a charismatic politician who has turned America into Christian theocracy which controls every aspect of life. The story follows a pregnant 17 year old who must hide from the violent Stormtroopers of God or she will find herself used for harvesting like an animal. Welcome to the Harvesting Room is in the tradition of Brave New World, The Wanting Seed, Clockwork Orange, and Hand Maid's Tale. If you like those, you will like Welcome to the Harvesting Room.

A collection of short stories about the dark and dirty underbelly of Post Industrial America. Homeless people try to carve out a life at Christmas, A Serial killer hides in plain sight helping the police to find the killer namely himself, A religious death cult, a husband commits murder-suicide, a rogue sheriff in the south kills anyone he doesn't like, these are just a few stories in this collection by Steven Farkas